The Blue Stone

The Blue Stone

by Richard Kennedy

DRAWINGS BY RONALD HIMLER

Holiday House · New York

Text copyright © 1976 by Richard Kennedy
Illustrations copyright © 1976 by Ronald Himler
Printed in the United States of America

Library of Congress Cataloging in Publication Data

Kennedy, Richard.
  The blue stone.
  SUMMARY: A blue stone which seems to have fallen from
heaven causes a farmer and his wife problems until they
learn how to carefully use its power.
  [1. Fairy tales] I. Himler, Ronald. II. Title.
PZ8.K387Bl [Fic]   76–9035
ISBN 0–8234–0283–5

For BOB DURAND,
*for remembering something
I had almost forgotten.*

Contents

Jack and Bertie

"You're a fool, Jack."

"Could be, Bertie, could be," said Jack. "There's a little truth in most all you say, darling."

Jack was in the stream bed, hitching up his trousers and poking around with his toes, turning rocks over.

"You're a dreamer, Jack."

"You're a beautiful woman, Bertie."

"I'm going back to the house, Jack. I can't stand your foolishment any longer."

"Please yourself, dear."

Bertie kept standing there. "Now what's all these birds fussing about for?"

Jack looked up. "Don't know, Bertie—seems more than ordinary, don't it? Swallows, ain't they?"

A dozen or more small birds were flocking about them and seemed to be concerned with Jack's efforts in the stream.

"You'll catch your death of cold in there splashering about," said Bertie, tucking her shawl a little closer under her arm. "There ain't no signs ever come down from heaven no more, least of all any meant for a ninny like yourself."

Jack straightened up and took a new hitch on his trousers. "Bertie, you should have seen it. It was just about the middle of the night, and I was laying awake looking out the window. And I saw this sparkle in the sky that took off like a shooting star, and it shot across the meadow. Then a little spark jumped off that star and fell down right here over the stream. I think I heard a sizzle when it hit the water. I tell you, it's some sort of a sign."

"Your noggin's loose, Jack," Bertie said. She watched him for a bit longer. "Well, I'll go put some soup on for you, honey. I wouldn't have you dying on my account."

"You ain't bad, Bertie," Jack said, and he watched his wife walk up the path toward the cottage, then continued muddling about in the stream bed.

Bertie hung a pot of soup over the fire and sat down with a piece of mending, and about the time the soup was starting to agitate she heard Jack shout out.

"Bertie, Bertie, I found it!"

He was running up to the cottage in his bare feet. Bertie shook her head and knocked on the side of the pot with the wooden spoon to chase any bad spirits out of it, then turned to watch Jack come slopping in the door.

"Mind, don't come slappering in and break your neck!"

"Look, Bertie," said Jack, pulling up a chair to the table. "It's a real part of a star from heaven, I swear it is!" He opened his hand. There in his palm lay what looked like a blue agate.

"Give it here," Bertie said, holding out the spoon. Jack put the stone in the spoon, and Bertie held it up close to her eyes. She sniffed, and ladled the stone out in front of her husband again, then turned to take the pot off the fire.

"You're a fool, Jack."

Jack rubbed the stone on his sleeve. He held it up to the window and peered through it. "Straight out of heaven it come, all lit up like the angels had been touching it, and it's got some blue sky in it yet." He put it up to his ear. "And I believe I can hear some harp music in it, and angels singing."

Bertie set the soup out and took a sip of hers, watching her husband.

"Bertie, it's a gift from Saint Peter himself I believe. Maybe a button off his very trousers. And them that finds these blue stones is more fortunate than all the kings in China."

"Let's see it again, Jack."

Jack handed it over, and Bertie popped it in her mouth.

"Bertie!" Jack cried.

"I believe it's a soup stone," Bertie said, "and I'm going to swallow it."

"Bertie, don't you dare!"

Bertie stuck out her tongue with the stone balanced on the end of it, then snatched it back in her mouth. "Hee, hee, hee," she laughed. Jack was wringing his hands. And then, though she didn't mean to do it really, she accidentally swallowed it.

And she turned into a chicken, sitting right there in the chair.

"Oh, Bertie!" Jack cried, and he tried to catch the chicken, but it ran into a corner where he couldn't get to it. "Oh, Bertie, my darling," Jack coaxed, "come out and we'll fix you back to yourself somehow." He made a clucking noise but the chicken wouldn't come out. So he got some grain and laid a path for it to follow along, and moved back so as not to frighten the bird. When the chicken came out eating the trail of grain, Jack made a jump at it, but only frightened it up onto a rafter.

"Bertie, my love, come down and finish your soup."

But it wouldn't, and at last Jack fetched a blanket and tossed it over the chicken and brought the chicken down in a bundle and hugged it and kissed it through the blanket. "Oh, Bertie, don't run away from me, I wouldn't hurt you for anything even if you was turned into a cockroach." He got a piece of string and reached up under the blanket and tied an end around the chicken's leg and let it hop out on the table.

"Bertie, you see what I told you? That stone you swallowed was something out of heaven, and you shouldn't make fun of signs. Now what we're to do, I don't know." The chicken appeared to be paying no attention and began pecking at a crack on the table. "Bertie, does you understand me, darling? Flap your wings, Bertie, if you got any sense."

But the chicken made no recognition, and Jack got up and walked around with his head in his hands. "All I can think of, Bertie, is to take you to the city tomorrow and see if we can't find someone to fix you back to your own self."

He got a box, then filled it with straw and stuck it near the fire and bedded down the chicken with plenty of feed and water. He wasn't hungry himself and sat at the table deeply worried, watching the chicken.

"Look, Bertie," Jack said. "I'll do your mending for you to entertain you, and I'll sing to you." He picked up the mending and sang to the chicken, which was resting comfortably. All the rest of the day he attended to comforting the chicken and trying to amuse it, and then it was time for bed. He knelt down and kissed the chicken on the head and said good night.

"One night as a chicken can't do much harm, Bertie," he said. "And maybe it has a meaning in it somewhere. If the worse happens, I'll build you the finest roost in the world. I love you, Bertie." Then Jack made off toward bed and presently was standing in the doorway in his underwear looking out toward the dark box. "I'm lonesome for you already, Bertie," he said, and then went to bed.

Of course he could hardly sleep. He dreamed of wild dogs and foxes and things that hurt chickens, and kept waking up to listen to the quiet house. A voice finally woke him when there was light in the sky. It was Bertie calling out, "Jack, you good-for-nothing, don't hog the blankets so!"

Jack leaped out of bed and ran to the kitchen, and there was Bertie lying cuddled up around the box trying to keep warm.

"Bertie! You're yourself!"

"I always thought I was," Bertie mumbled. "Now let loose of the blanket."

Jack got down on the floor and hugged her until she started slapping at his face and saying, "Let me be, let me be, what's got into you anyhow?" And then she came wide awake and sat up and looked around. Jack

wrapped her up in a blanket and she remembered slowly and started crying.

"Oh, Jack, it was awful. I was changed into a chicken. I remember you was there, and talking to me, but it was like a spoon clappering inside a bowl, and I couldn't understand anything, and I was afraid of being stewed. And Jack, the racket that goes on in a chicken's head you wouldn't put up with."

"I know, dumpling, I know," Jack said, and he got a fire going and battered up some dough for breakfast cakes. "You must be hungry, darling, seeing as you only had a scatter of grain for supper. There's a bit of milk in the pitcher, looks churny but it's good. Wish we had an egg for you, darling."

And then he just naturally looked over to the box, and there in the straw was an egg.

"Bertie! You laid an egg!"

"No! Did I?"

Jack took the egg to the table. "Sure as anything, Bertie, look!"

"Stars and moons, Jack, I really did!"

"You did a beautiful job, Bertie. I never seen an egg so lovely."

"Aw, you're just saying that, Jack."

"Bertie, I never lie to you—it's just the most perfect egg I've ever seen." He held it up to the light to admire it. "What's this? Why, Bertie, I believe it's got something inside of it."

Then at the same time they looked at each other and said, "The stone!"

"Of course!" said Jack. "That's exactly how you became yourself again, by laying out that blue stone into an egg."

"You know, Jack, I had a feeling inside like I was doing something but couldn't figure out what it was."

"Oh, Bertie, it's wonderful. Now we have an egg for breakfast and the stone back again."

"You don't mean to *eat* the egg, do you? Why, Jack, that would be like eating one of my own children. I couldn't do it, never."

Jack thought on it for a moment. "I suppose you're right, dear. Look—you wouldn't want it to go rotten, either, and we can't throw it away with the stone in it, so I'll boil it. It'll be safekeeping from breaking that way and we'll think what to do about it as time goes by."

"You're not *always* a fool, Jack."

Jack put the egg in the teapot to boil. They ate breakfast then, and Bertie told Jack more of what it was like to be a chicken.

"They's awful clumsy and awkward critters, Jack. Why, it was all I could do to keep my balance. Like walking around on a pair of rickety stilts, it was. And pecking—why, it about jolted my brains loose to do it, but I just had to, you know, since it was my nature. And they can't fly worth beans, if you want to know about that. A person don't know how lucky he is, Jack." Bertie sipped at her tea. "Why, it's a blessing just to have lips."

Jack touched her hand and said, "I'm so happy you're not a chicken no more, Bertie."

"Well, it's a great load off my mind, Jack, and that's true."

When the egg was boiled, Jack cooled it in some water and set it in a little dish on a high shelf. They looked at it in wonder.

"Maybe that's what it was for," Jack said, "just to remind us how lucky we are to be people."

"It's a relief, I can tell you that," said Bertie. "A chicken's got no more sense than a scrap sheet."

That night Jack was at work carving a new latch for the door. There was talk around that a robber was in the neighborhood. Bertie was looking in a little mirror as she brushed her hair.

"Jack," she said, laying her hands in her lap. "I'm getting old and wrinkling all up."

"Bertie, you ain't half old yet, and them wrinkles just helps me feel how pretty you are in the dark."

Bertie smiled and continued to brush her hair. Then she stopped again. "Jack?"

"Aye, turnip?"

"What kind of chicken did I look like?"

Jack looked at her. "Bertie, you was the prettiest looking chicken I ever saw in my life."

"You're just saying that."

"Bertie, I never seen such a fine looking chicken.

You made my mouth water."

"Aw, you're a fool, Jack."

"I love you, Bertie," Jack said, and went on to carving some more.

Mockersheep

Jack rolled out of bed and pulled on his trousers. Bertie was up, setting on some oat mush for breakfast.

"Bertie," said Jack. "If you went and borrowed a bit of salt pork from sister Minn, we could promise it back when it comes killing time for the pig."

"Oh, Jack, I hates to think about it—it's just my favorite pig of all."

"Time comes for everyone," said Jack.

"Aye," said Bertie. She went to the window and looked at the pig down in its slop pen. She thought a minute. "What do you suppose happens when a pig dies, Jack?"

"It gets et by folks, same as we get et by worms."

"Jack, you needn't remind me! And I don't mean that. I mean what happens to its soul?"

"I dunno, Bertie. It gets et by people's souls, I suppose. Will you go ask sister Minn for some salt pork?"

"Going, Jack," said Bertie, and she put on her shawl and went out and down the path and across the road to sister Minn's place. Jack stirred the oat mush slowly and talked to himself. "Course then what happens to worms' souls? Suppose we do eat pigs' souls, then do worms eat our souls?" Jack shook his head. "Can't be. That'd make heaven full of worms, then. If it was like that, nobody'd bother going there."

"I ain't bothering," said a voice. Jack turned his head. The door was open, and a dark figure was standing just inside and in the shadows. A hand holding a dagger crossed the opening and caught hold of the door and shut it slowly and quietly.

"Set easy," said the man, and he stepped silently over to Jack and put the point of the dagger at his throat. "I likes people what think about heaven and pray and such," said the man. "Makes it easier to sneak up on 'em." The man glanced out the window and around the hut. He was thick waisted and muscular, with stringy black hair and a corner of his mouth tucked into a permanent smirk. He wore a sleeveless leather jerkin with brass studs on it. "Yer heard about me?" he asked.

"The robber that's been about?" said Jack.

"Yers truly. Mockersheep is the name. Yer know how many bones I broke lately?"

Jack wanted to make the man feel proud and at ease. "Two score?"

Mockersheep laughed. "Come nearly," he said. "Where's yer woman?"

"Gone for a bit," Jack said. "You can take what you want and leave."

Mockersheep went to the window. He stepped quickly to the side of the door and laid back against the wall. Bertie pushed the door open in a minute and walked inside. "I spoke to the pig as I passed, Jack," she said. "I told him he was going to heaven soon, and he appeared comforted."

Mockersheep closed the door behind her. "Yer going too, mum, if yer ain't careful now."

"Land!" Bertie cried.

"This is Mr. Mockersheep," Jack said.

"The robber!"

"Yers truly. Yer heard of me, eh? But yer stupid like all the rest." The robber went to the window and opened it and spit. He stood there holding his dagger toward Bertie and Jack, gazing out over the King's roadway. "Stupid like all the rest, thinking robbing is all I'm about. They think all I love is gold, just like their own miserable selves, and it's cause they's stupid and never thought things out." He turned to face them. "Don't yer know, it ain't gold what makes a man happy."

"I never believed it was," said Bertie.

"Then yer got some brains anyhow," said Mockersheep. He pulled Bertie to the window. "Look down in that bunch of trees. My horse is down in there, a big dapple mare. Yer go get her, put her in the shed. Get!" He pushed Bertie to the door, and she went running out.

"Serve up that mush, man," Mockersheep said to Jack. The robber took up the salt pork Bertie had dropped on the table and chawed on it, then went to slopping up the mush Jack gave him. Presently Bertie came back in. Mockersheep turned with his dagger in hand. "Set," he said. Bertie sat with Jack at the other side of the table.

Mockersheep talked as he ate. "They's all stupid, and that's why they'll never catch me. They's always looking for somebody that robs for gold, just like they'd do themselves if they wasn't mewly dogs. Sure, I take gold when I find it. I ain't ignorant. But that ain't it. Believe me, I seen rich people in my time, seen lords and ladies dressed in silk and jewels, I have, and was they happy? Never that I saw. They's all just as fretful and frightened as beggars, but they don't like to show it. What's that egg?" Mockersheep pointed to the egg in the dish up on the shelf.

"Just an old egg," said Bertie.

"Give it here." He took the egg from Jack. "Hard or raw?"

"Hard," Jack said.

Mockersheep cracked the egg on his forehead and began peeling it.

"Stupid," he said. "And I'd be as stupid as them if I was thinking gold could make a man happy. Naw, gold never does it. It's what's inside a man what makes him happy, something deep inside him he got to satisfy that makes a man happy. D'yer get my meaning?"

"I believe it's so," said Bertie. Jack nodded.

"They can take gold away from yer," Mockersheep continued. "Then yer ain't got anything again and yer miserable. What a man's got to do is build on something nobody can take away from him. Something inside." He thumped his chest. "D'yer get my meaning?"

"Like having children and caring for them," said Bertie.

"Like doing work that satisfies you," said Jack.

"Aye," said Mockersheep. "Only for me it's breaking bones. I'm glad yer understand and won't complain when the time comes. Have yer got a decent club I can use?"

Just then there was the rumble of horses down the road.

Mockersheep stood up, clutching the egg in one hand, his dagger in the other.

"That horse in the shed?"

"Aye," Bertie said.

Mockersheep went to the window. "They's coming up here!" He looked around, then strode over to a closet and kicked a bucket and mop out of it. "Yer lucky," he said to Jack and Bertie. "Yer got a chance not to get yer bones broke, though it's hard for me to keep a promise like that. Them are King's men coming, but yer don't give me up and I won't break yer bones afterwards. That's all." He shut the closet door on himself just as the horses outside came up.

There came a pounding on the door. "King's men," a voice called out. Jack went and opened the door. A big man with gold stripes on his coat stood there. "King's business. Captain Cupper here." He pushed the door farther open and walked inside past Jack. "You, woman," said the Captain, "a bucket of water for the horses." Bertie went out back to draw a bucket. Captain Cupper looked about and sat down at the table. He had his sword drawn and laid it across his knees.

"There's a man we're after," he said, "and the dog'll be robbing somewhere hereabouts." Jack was sitting with his back to the closet. Mockersheep could be out in a leap and at his throat. "You seen anyone strange about?" the Captain asked.

"No, sir," said Jack. "What's his looks?"

"Folks give it different—'bout your size, I should say. Do you have any fresh meat? King's business. You don't, huh? What's this—egg peelings? Give us some eggs, then, King's business. . . . No? No more eggs, just this slop in the bowl here? Well, I suppose we can wait."

Bertie came back in and sat down.

"Bertie, the King's men want a bit of food."

"Cabbage and potatoes," said Bertie, getting up.

"No fresh meat?"

"No meat, sir."

Bertie got the cabbage and potatoes simmering.

Captain Cupper inspected the edge of his sword. "'Bout your size," he repeated. "Rides a big dapple mare, that's how you'd know him. Mockersheep he calls himself. Breaks bones, he does, after robbing what he can. Blasted strange! We try to trap him with gold, and he goes and robs somebody for pennies and breaks their bones even when they're obliging. Can't figure him out nohow."

"Is there a reward for him, sir?" Bertie asked.

"For Mockersheep?" said the Captain. "No, mum, no reward for Mockersheep at all. The king don't want him. But there's a reward for his head. Ha, ha, ha, ha!" The Captain laughed at his joke and slapped his knee. "Yes, mum. There's a reward for his head. You know how much? All the gold pieces you can stuff in a goat's bladder, and choose your own goat. That's what. And you know what's more? What's more is that I myself had a dream that I was going to get his head, and how's that? There's others out after Mockersheep, but it was me that had that dream. How do you say on that?"

"Dreams is signs, sometimes," said Jack.

There was a clatter and the closet door squeaked. Captain Cupper gripped his sword on ready as the door slowly began to swing open. A duck waddled out and said "Quack, quack, qu——" just before the Captain shouted "Hi!" and with a swing of his sword lopped its head clean off its body.

"Whoops!" Bertie said.

"Fresh meat," said the Captain, as he jammed the tip of his sword into the body of the duck and lifted it over to Bertie. "King's business. You oughtn't to lie to the King's men, woman."

Bertie held the duck tenderly and laid it on a board and began to pluck it. Jack got up to take a look at it, then he opened the closet all the way. A pile of clothes was on the floor, and the dagger laying there.

Bertie got the duck plucked and cleaned and cooked up with the cabbage and potatoes, and the King's men ate their fill.

"Remember," said Captain Cupper, getting ready to leave. "This fellow rides a big dapple mare, that's how you'd know him—ain't sure what he looks like at all, some says one way, some says another. But his head is worth gold. Thank 'ee, mum, for the meat and such." The Captain touched his forehead with his knuckles in a salute, then he was gone with his men. Bertie and Jack sat down at the table and looked at the duck's head where it lay. The duck's beak gleamed like gold where it caught the sun.

The Moon

The King's men had been gone an hour. Bertie had dug the blue stone out of the duck's guts and it was laying on the table next to the duck's head.

"Do you honest mean to do it, Jack?"

"Why, certain, Bertie. It's a gift from heaven for us, the blue stone is. It's all because of it we got this duck's head, worth a goat's bladder full of gold coins."

"It don't look like much, Jack. Do you think the King'll give you all that gold for an old duck's head?"

"It ain't just a duck's head, Bertie—it's that robber's head, Mockersheep's, and that's how it's worth something. And even if it don't look much like him, we got his horse for proof, and the blue stone to prove it out finally, if it comes to that."

"How would that be, Jack?"

"Why, all they got to do is feed the stone to somebody, then they'd see it was the truth how it changes a person."

Bertie set her chin on her hand. "I don't know, Jack."

"You'll see, Bertie." Jack got out a little leather bag and stuffed the duck's head in it, then dropped the blue stone in after it. He got up. "Bertie, I'll be back in a fine wagon, just you wait."

They went out back and led Mockersheep's big mare from the shed, and Jack took the reins. He kissed Bertie. "Now don't worry and don't mope around concerning about me. Go visit sister Minn and tell her we'll give her back a whole pig for that hunk of salt pork." He paused and looked at their goat.

"What are you thinking, Jack?"

"I was figuring, Bertie, if I ought to take a goat's bladder with me."

"No, Jack, I wouldn't let you do it."

"Aye. She's scrawny anyhow. I'll choose one of the King's goats."

He kissed Bertie again and headed off on the King's roadway toward the city. Bertie watched him go up and over a far hill, wiping her hands in her apron with worry. Then she headed down toward sister Minn's place to tell her the whole story and try to act like she thought everything was fine. She didn't, though.

But Jack was feeling good. He was gone a mile or so when he stopped to get a drink from the stream alongside the road. He sat there a minute on his hands and knees looking in the water and dreaming about how rich Bertie and him were going to be. Then it was like a tree had fallen on him. He was flattened out and his head was thrust into the mud. Weights were on his arms and legs, and then one arm was turned up hard against his back, and there was snarling and cussing in his ears.

"Now, you scroggy scrubber, now you'll pay!"

"Tie the blugger up, get him on his feet!"

"Get his bloody dagger away from him, hold his bloody arms!"

Jack was jerked to his feet. Mud was in his eyes, but he could squint and see he had been jumped by some of the King's men, four of them, different ones than had come to the cottage. They whipped his arms around in front of him and tied his wrists with thongs, all the while jolting him in the head and taking turns kicking his legs and knocking him about.

"Bring him up here," a captain yelled from the roadway, and Jack was led up out of the stream bed.

"Hah!" said the Captain. "We got ya finally, didn't we, ya skuggy dog!"

Jack knew what it was. Because of the big dapple mare, they thought that he was Mockersheep.

"I ain't him!" Jack cried.

"Ain't who?" said the Captain.

"Mockersheep, I ain't him!"

"Yah, in a pig's satchel ya ain't." The Captain got down off his horse and drew his sword. "Fetch him over to yonder stump, men."

They drug Jack over to a tree stump and forced him down on his knees next to it. One of the men grabbed his hair from the other side of the stump and plunked his head on it sideways. Another ripped his shirt and laid bare his neck.

"I was going to see the King," Jack pleaded. "I was taking him Mockersheep's head."

"Yar, well nevermind that, we'll take it for ya and say ya sent it. It'll save ya the trip."

Jack knew he didn't have a chance to explain. The Captain planted his feet apart and took the sword in both hands.

"Last words!" Jack cried. "Last words!"

"Yar, I suppose," said the Captain. "Say and be done with it."

"A man ought to get a last meal. You know that's so. And all I want's a bite, just a taste before you cuts my head off."

"We ain't sparing no food for the likes of ya," the Captain said.

"Let my head up a little. I got a bite to eat here with me. Bad luck if you don't."

"Aw, let him up a little," said the Captain. The men loosened their hold and Jack took the little leather bag from his belt.

The Captain eyed him suspiciously. "Careful, now," he said.

Jack dug in the bag and took out the duck's head.

"Ugh! I knew ya was a rotten dog, but eating a *duck's* head. Ugh!"

Jack laid the head on the stump and dug to the bottom of the bag and got his fingers on the blue stone. Then before they could see a thing he dashed it up and into his mouth and swallowed it.

And he was a duck.

His clothes fell from him and he sprang off flapping and quacking between some legs and down the bank to the stream. He fled over the water, running and swimming and flying, and off across a field and into some woods. This while, the King's men stood around yelling and cussing at each other about what happened and claiming the others had gone crazy because each thought he'd gone crazy himself, seeing a man turn into a duck. And only after a bit did they come to agree it had happened and was magic, and decided to give chase, but by then the duck was out of sight and lost to them.

Jack, the duck, hid in the woods till it started getting dark, and tried to collect his thoughts, but could only think in quacks and couldn't understand the language. Except he did know he had to wait till dark and then get

home. The moon was starting to come up when he left the woods.

He ran on back to the stream, then up and across the King's roadway after looking carefully both ways for any King's men who might be out. He ran hard for a while, then, and almost stumbled onto a couple of men sitting on a cart at the side of the road smoking their pipes. They were talking. Jack hid in some brush.

"They's gone mad, I tell you!"

"It's the moon," said the second man, indicating the full moon with the stem of his pipe.

"I don't know about that, but they's gone mad. They come riding up and without no word they chased down six of my ducks and chopped their heads off. Then they just stood there looking at the carcasses a while and rode off. They did the same over at Amos's place and all up and down the road I hear."

"They don't say nothing?"

"Well, they's cussing all the time, of course, being King's men, and calling the poor ducks dirty dogs and scurvy robbers and such like. They's mad, I tell you."

"Probably," said the second man. "I figure it's the moon."

"Either that or the end of the world."

"One or the other," said the second, sucking on his pipe.

Jack cut around the men and ran on and got to the cottage door in another ten minutes. He clobbered at the door with his head and beat his wings on it. Bertie opened it.

"Now what's all this?"

Jack ran inside under her legs and jumped from table to chair, generally banging himself around the place, upsetting bowls and boxes and making a terriffic amount of quacking and squalling. Bertie took up a broom and started swinging at him and knocked things about this way and that. She tired before she could bash him and sat down for a minute to rest. Jack gave up flapping and crashing about, which wasn't proving anything and was likely to get him brained. Then he did the right thing. He went to the closet and sat down in amongst Mockersheep's clothing and just sat there looking at Bertie pitifully, nudging his beak into a shirtsleeve and looking at Bertie to understand.

She was still catching her breath. "I'll slam you good next time, just you wait," she said, and she got up slow and meaningful and edged up on the duck with the broom ready. Then she caught on.

"Jack!" she cried, dropping the broom. "Is it yourself? Oh, Jack, you et the stone, didn't you? Jack, why'd you do it?" She picked the duck up and set it on the table to study the problem. "You can't lay an egg, Jack, you know you can't do that. It wouldn't be proper and gentlemanly." She thought for a while. "You'll have to trust me, Jack. Try to remember you're just a dumb beast and I know what's best, no matter what happens."

She got some twine and tied it around the duck's feet. She laid it on its side while she made a good knot and let out another long end of twine. She hummed to the duck to keep it calm. Then she hung the duck upside down from a rafter and wrung its neck while she beat it with a stick, and out plopped the blue stone onto the floor, and in a second afterwards Jack came pitching down after it, naked as a snake, and knocked himself out completely.

Bertie put a wet rag on his head and covered him with a quilt. The blue stone she set on the table and for a long while sat watching Jack. Then she went to bed.

Adrian

Jack lay in bed all the next day and Bertie cared for him. She sat and held his hand and listened to his story.

"And Bertie, I'm just so sore all over from being kicked and knocked about and having my neck stretched out by them and then wrung by you and beat by yourself, too, and falling on my head—I honest think we ought to throw that blue stone back in the stream where I found it and let heaven help someone else out for a while. I'm tired of it."

"It's been a misery for you, Jack darling, but that's because we didn't know what that stone was for. It's got miracles in it, sure, and all we got to do is find out how to use it. Now when I told sister Minn how it changed people into ducks and chickens and such, she pulled at that long hair on her nose and seemed to remember something, and what she remembered is that she heard one of those singing men, those minstrels, singing out a song about such a stone, right there in the city not only last week."

Jack came up on an elbow. "Well, then, what did he sing?"

"Sister Minn says she can't remember. She said it was a song about ducks and chickens and things falling out of heaven, all about the blue stone and how it's supposed to be if you find one."

"Just so?"

"Near as she remembered. She tried to get the words of the song up but couldn't—pulled that nose hair right out thinking on it."

So Jack and Bertie decided he'd have to go to the city and hunt up the minstrel and hear the song about the blue stone. He lay in bed for a day more before his bones felt well enough to make the walk. Bertie packed some dinner for him, and he tied up a blanket to sling over his shoulder in case he should have to spend a night on the road, or in the city. Then he took their savings, just a few coppers, and made to leave. Bertie straightened his collar and patted his buttons.

"Be careful, Jack, and you're sure the King's men won't know you?"

"I had mud all over my face, Bertie."

"Now mind, if you see the King and Queen, fill up your eyes with it. I want to know just everything about how they look, and what the Queen was wearing, and does she have tiny feet, and all you can remember, Jack."

"Aye, Bertie." He stood ready to go. Bertie looked him over once more and then kissed him, and he was off. They waved at each other when Jack turned off onto the King's roadway. Bertie started humming to herself and fixing things up around the house.

Jack passed and greeted people on the road but saw no King's men. It was late afternoon when he arrived in the city. He walked up and down several winding streets asking where he might find the minstrel man, and at last found a dusty boy in a rag of a jacket who could tell him. First, the boy looked him up and down very careful. He had a wily way about him.

"For a penny, sir, I'll tell you where to find him."

Jack tossed him a penny.

"Over in yonder inn, in the alehouse most like. Another penny, and I'll sing you a song myself."

"Do you know one about a blue stone?"

"I know one about a blue dog."

"Thank you all the same," said Jack and headed for the inn, which was called the Silver Plate. He went into the alehouse.

Jack stood for a minute till his eyes got used to the darkness inside, and then he saw his man without asking for him. He was thin, with long sandy hair parted in the middle and a moustache that hung down on the ends nearly to his chin. A lute was sitting on the table, and he was taking a gulp off a large tankard when Jack walked up to him. The man wiped his mouth with the back of his hand and cocked an eyebrow at Jack.

"Are you friendly to the people's cause, sir?" he said.

"I . . . I think I am," said Jack, not knowing what the man meant, but he liked people and supposed it was something about that.

"Sit, then. And if you wasn't, we could toast the King. But let's do that anyway. Innkeeper!" The innkeeper, a bald and bulgy man in an apron, came over with two tankards of ale. The minstrel waited for Jack to pay for them, then he lifted his tankard. Jack did so, too. "A toast to the King," said the minstrel, "that he may be toasted better later on." He winked at Jack and took a deep draught of his ale. Jack drank too.

"Do you know the King?" asked Jack, mindful of the news Bertie wanted.

"Aye, I know him," said the man. He licked his forefinger and snapped some spit on the floor.

"What's he like, then?"

"An oaf, sir, an oaf. You have the word of one who knows grace."

"And the Queen?"

"Ugly. You have the word of a man who loves beauty. But you didn't come up so directly for that news. What's your business?"

"My name is Jack, and my wife Bertie and me . . ."

The man put out his hand. His sleeve was patched with different colored cloths. "Adrian is my name, sir, as honest a man as they come nowadays, and that is no compliment to myself."

"I come for a song," Jack said, "a song about a blue stone."

"Ah, yes," said Adrian, "a blue stone. He took another long drink, then reached for his lute. He looked out the window for a bit, moving his lips quietly. "Hmmmmmmmmm. How about if it's a blue rock, Jack? I can get more rhymes out of rock than stone."

"But I didn't want you to make up a song," Jack said. "I thought you knew a song about a blue stone, and that's what I was after."

"No. No, I don't. But I'd be pleased to learn it, Jack. How does it go?"

"Ah, I don't know either," said Jack, putting his head in his hands. "An old lady said she heard you singing a song about a blue stone, with ducks and chickens in it also."

"I'm sorry, Jack," said Adrian, "but I don't know such a song." He took a gulp of his ale. "But here's one about a blue dog you might like," and he strummed his lute.

"No, not that," said Jack. "Are there others in the city like yourself?"

"Minstrels? No, I'm the only one right now. It's a

poor city."

Jack finished up his ale. "It's been nice, anyway," he said.

"My pleasure, sir," said Adrian and began strumming softly on his lute as Jack walked away. He was almost to the door when Adrian called out, "Wait a minute. Come back!" Jack returned to the table. "Did you say this song had chickens and ducks in it?"

"Aye, it should."

"Well, I do know a song with chickens and ducks in it. Not so much a real song—more like a riddle, I've always thought. But it goes like this." Adrian stroked a chord and sang, " 'When heaven is falling the pieces are blue . . .' "

"That's it, that's it!" Jack cried.

"What? How can you know that, I haven't even come to the chickens and ducks yet."

"Go on, go on," Jack said.

Adrian began again:

When heaven is falling, the pieces are blue,
and under your tongue, a poem will come true,
if man be the first to find it but heed,
nor use it in vengeance nor anger nor greed.

But heaven is not for the swallows of men,
a duck for a man, for a woman a hen,
but swallows for swallows and wings for the new,
born of the angels, the pieces are blue.

Jack sat so earnestly silent at hearing it that Adrian didn't say anything, just continued strumming quietly and looking out the window.

"It's hard to understand," said Jack.

"Aye," Adrian said. "It's an ancient song. A very old man taught it to me, and he himself was taught by an old man."

"But what does it mean?" asked Jack.

"I don't know and the old man didn't know. But somebody will, somehow, somewhere, so I sing it now and again. It's like carrying a message around with you, with no address you see, but it'll find its way to who it should." Adrian looked at Jack with great curiosity then. "Do you know what it means?"

Jack rubbed his chin. "Parts of it. I can tell you that the pieces of heaven are blue stones, I know that. And then that part about swallows and men . . ."

" 'But heaven is not for the swallows of men'?"

"That's it. Those aren't birdlike swallows, but that means that you shouldn't swallow one of these stones."

"Oh? And why's that?"

"Because if you do swallow one of these stones, you turn into a duck, and a woman turns into a hen."

"Ahhhhhh," said Adrian.

"But the rest of it I don't know," said Jack. "Could you learn it to me?"

"Certainly," Adrian said. He beckoned to the inn-keeper and recited to Jack. "We'll take it two lines at a time. First this: 'When heaven is falling the pieces are blue, and under your tongue a poem will come true.' "

Jack repeated the lines, and they sat there drinking and saying the song back and forth for a time. It was dark out now, and Adrian closed the shutter on the window. The innkeeper came over once and touched Adrian on the shoulder. Adrian looked up and nodded and continued teaching Jack the song.

Then the door burst open, and the same young boy that had told Jack where to find Adrian jumped inside and yelled out "Zork's man, Zork's man!" and jumped out again.

Adrian took a last quick gulp of his drink and flung open the shutter and window. He grabbed his lute by the neck and hopped nimbly up on the table and put a leg out the window. He turned and said to Jack, "Have you got it now?"

Jack nodded. "But what's happening?"

Adrian winked and dropped lightly to the ground. The innkeeper took the empty tankard and made a quick wipe of the table where Adrian had been sitting. Hardly had he finished this when a large dark figure thumped through the door. The three or four other men in the place hunched themselves around their tankards and tried to seem like they weren't paying anything any mind, but the place was heavy with nervousness. It was Zork's man. He had a broad face and his eyes glinted deep in their sockets like rats running around in a dun-

geon. The glints fell on Jack. The man walked over and put his knuckles against Jack's head and turned his face to get a look at him.

The innkeeper came over. "He's just a country man, come in for drinking is all."

The large man snorted like he didn't believe it, and looked at the open window. He wiped a finger on the table where Adrian had been sitting, and put the back of his hand to the bench to feel if it was warm. Then he looked carefully at Jack again and went around behind him. He circled his great hands lightly around Jack's throat and said, "Whoever next sees that songbird, tell him I want him to sing the frog's song for me. It goes like this—CROAK! CROAK! CROAK!" At each "croak" the man tightened his stranglehold, and when he let go, Jack gasped and slumped on his bench. The man turned and went out without another word.

The innkeeper sat down. "Are you all right?"

"Aye," said Jack, "but my neck's getting some hard wear these days. Who was that?"

"Zork's man. Zork's the King's magician or sorcerer or whatever you might call it. But call it what you will, he's no good anyway, losing his powers and getting into blackmail, and making honest folk pay protection money and such. And worse. A bad fellow. Now he's after Adrian because of some little songs Adrian has been making up and passing around. Adrian makes people laugh at Zork, and Zork wants to kill him."

He closed the window and looked toward the door. "You'd better go, but I wouldn't stay in the city if I was you. Walk wide around corners and get out on the roadway and you'll be all right. I believe he thought you were a friend of Adrian."

Jack took up his blanket roll. The innkeeper went out the door and whispered loudly, "Pin! Pin!" He came back to Jack. "Follow the lad. He knows the best way to the gates." He put his hand on Jack's shoulder. "Godspeed, friend."

When Jack came out the boy turned and skipped up the street. Jack had to trot to keep up with him. Dark and careful cats crouched in wonder to see people moving along the night streets as quickly and slyly as themselves.

Poetry

The boy left Jack at the city gate, and Jack walked the King's roadway for an hour before he dared to bed down. He slept cold, then very early took to the road again. Over and over he recited the song about the blue stone, and his excitement grew as he believed he had solved most of the rhyme.

The sun was only a cockcrow high when Jack arrived home. He entered quietly, but Bertie awoke when he neared the bed.

"Shhhh," said Jack, putting a finger to her lips. "I've got to sleep, love, but I've learned the song about the blue stone. Sister Minn was right—there was a minstrel named Adrian, and Zork's man was after him . . . and other things. But I've got to sleep now, love."

Bertie was impatient to know everything, but she let Jack sleep two hours before holding a cup of hot broth under his nose. Jack sipped the broth and munched a crust of bread while he told Bertie the story.

"Oh, Jack, you're lucky to be alive."

Jack piled out of bed and pulled on his clothes. "Where's the stone, Bertie?"

Bertie got the stone and Jack studied it at the table with even greater interest than ever.

"Now, do you understand the words of the song, Bertie?"

Bertie folded her hands in front of her like a schoolgirl. "Tell me again, Jack."

"Well, some of it's plain enough. The first line says, 'When heaven is falling the pieces are blue.' Of course the stone is one of those pieces." Bertie nodded. "Then the part of it that says, 'but heaven is not for the swallows of men, a duck for man, for a woman a hen'—that part we know from what's already happened. It just means that nobody ought to swallow one of these pieces of heaven—one of these blue stones—because of changing into a duck or a chicken."

"That's the truth, Jack."

"But now listen, Bertie," said Jack, laying his hands

flat on either side of the stone. "Here's the first part complete:

When heaven is falling, the pieces are blue
and under your tongue, a poem will come true,
if man be the first to find it but heed,
nor uses it in anger, nor vengeance, nor greed.

There, do you see it, Bertie?"

Bertie frowned. "Not all, Jack, but it sounds like a warning. Maybe we shouldn't have tried to get that gold off the stone's working, since it was from heaven and all."

"Right, Bertie, I believe it's so, since you might call that greed. But still it's wonderful, Bertie. It sounds to me like the song says that if you put the stone in your mouth—under your tongue—then whatever poem you say will come true! Open your mouth, Bertie."

Bertie did, and Jack dropped the stone in.

"Careful and don't swallow it. Put it under your tongue. Can you talk, darling?"

"Aye, it lays there nice."

"Now, Bertie, you're to say a poem, and we'll see if it comes true."

"A lullaby, Jack?"

"No, Bertie, that wouldn't do it. It might just make us fall asleep and there's not much to that. Make up a poem, Bertie."

"Ah, Jack, I can't hardly do that."

"Sure you can, Bertie. Just try and think of something now and I will, too."

Jack got up and walked around the table several times with his arms behind his back. Bertie sat with her eyes shut squinty-tight and her hands clasped in her lap, thinking. "Quork! Quork!" Their pig nosed open the door and Jack was about to shoo it out when he thought better and said "soooooo, pig, sooooooo," sweetly, and the pig came in.

"Bertie, make up a poem on the pig. There's lots of words that go with pig—big, dig, fig, sprig, swig . . . ."

Bertie opened her eyes and concentrated on the pig. Jack got it a cob to make it stand still.

"I don't get nothing, Jack," Bertie said, breaking off a crust of bread from the loaf on the table. She put it on the floor for the pig. "Jack . . . ?"

"Aye?"

"What was it Adrian said about the King?"

"He didn't like the King, Bertie. He didn't say much."

"What did he call him, though?"

"An oaf, dear, and called the Queen ugly."

"Hmmmmmmmm," said Bertie. "Can the poem be silly, Jack?"

"Aye. It's only to see if we're right about how the stone works."

Bertie nodded her head up and down several times

like she was keeping time, then she said, "I've got it, Jack." And she said a silly poem:

> *The Queen is ugly,*
> *and the King is an oaf,*
> *and this poem might change*
> *a pig to a loaf.*

And right in front of their eyes the pig disappeared as fast as a balloon popping, and where it had been was a large loaf of bread.

"It worked, Bertie! It worked!" Jack hugged Bertie and inspected the loaf, and it was real bread. After their excitement died down, they agreed that even if it was magic, it was all in all something of a loss. The pig was worth more than the loaf. However, they decided that if one poem could change a pig to a loaf, another might change it back again, and to this end Bertie and Jack worked at making up a new poem, and at last they had it. Bertie, with the blue stone under her tongue, said the poem at the loaf of bread.

> *The King is wise,*
> *and the Queen is pretty,*
> *and this poem might change*
> *a loaf to a piggy.*

And they had their pig back again.

"Darling!" said Bertie and kissed it, then poked it out the door and got some flour and a couple of pans out of the cupboard. She was going to bake some bread.

It was true. The blue stone had the magic in it to change anything in the world to anything else if only you could make up a poem to say how you wanted it to be.

> *. . . but heed,*
> *nor use it in anger, nor vengeance, nor greed.*

It was early in the day yet when Bertie called Jack in from the garden. She had two fresh loaves of bread cooling in the window.

"Is it greed, Jack, for us to give a pig to sister Minn?"

"Why no, Bertie, that's a gift. That's a nice thing to do."

"And how about if we make a pig for ourselves, Jack?"

Jack pulled on his ear and thought. "Just one, Bertie? No, I think that would be all right. Greed means wanting to get a whole lot of things for yourself, more than you need. It'd ease life a little having another pig. I don't think you could call that greed."

"Good!" Bertie set the two loaves on the floor and said the correct poem first at one loaf, then the other, and they had two fine plump pigs. "Do you suppose, Jack, if I'd put cloves in the bread, the pigs would already be seasoned?"

Jack had no idea on that and went out to work in the garden. He was puzzling on the song of the blue stone—the two last lines that he hadn't figured out:

But swallows for swallows and wings for the new,
born of the angels, the pieces are blue.

Over and over he said the words to himself, and would stop and lean on his hoe and look off in the distance for a while, then shake his head and go back to work.

Bertie tied a blue ribbon on the tail of sister Minn's pig and put a rope around its neck. She hefted the other pig up against her side and led off on down the path. After she dropped their own pig into the slop pen, she crossed the roadway and headed over to sister Minn's with her gift pig.

Sister Minn was angry. She was delighted with the gift pig but got to grumbling again soon about one of her neighbors, an old lady who lived on the other side of the fence, called the Old Magger. She was a strange and scratchy old lady who always wore a hood to stay out of the light. Some said she lived on toadstools and nothing else, and she was always rummaging in the woods, picking at the ground and at the trees, collecting bones of little animals, tearing bird nests apart for a few twigs she wanted, trapping squirrels and cutting off their tails, and digging up roots. Some nights she sat and carried on hooting conversations with owls. She lived in a dirty shack and had a few pigs which she let run and root where they could. One of them had got through the fence and rooted up sister Minn's garden. That's why sister Minn was angry. But it didn't do to argue with the Old Magger. She was full of threats and would cook up some sort of potion to use against anyone who crossed her. She knew some dark things, and people were afraid of her, but folks now and then in desperation would go to her for help. For the payment of a basket of vegetables, they might come away with a small bottle of green liquid or a twisted root that would change somebody's mind or health.

And so because sister Minn was angry at the Old Magger, Bertie was too, and now she had a little bit of magic herself. Therefore, when she left sister Minn's, she walked along the fence until she came upon one of the Old Magger's pigs, and she changed it into a loaf of bread. "That'll teach her," Bertie said and chuckled.

She was walking along the roadpath when along came a farmer from the opposite direction. He was carrying a suckling pig wrapped in a blanket, taking it to sell in the city marketplace. It was narrow there, and he bumped Bertie off the path into the ditch and hadn't time to beg her pardon. Bertie was about to cuss him but then changed her mind.

"Good farmer," Bertie said from the ditch. "Sir, is that a suckling pig you have there?"

"Aye," said the man. He stopped, hoping to save himself a journey to the city. "Do you want to buy a pig?"

Bertie pulled herself out of the ditch and approached the man.

"Is his nose pink? Is his eyes clear?" she asked.

"Look for yourself," said the man.

Bertie took the blue stone from her apron pocket and put it under her tongue. Then she lifted a fold of the blanket and looked in on the pig. She put her head down near to it and whispered. She folded the blanket back in place.

"No thank you, I think not," she said. "He looks a bit rude."

"Bah!" said the man and strode off.

Bertie was laughing when she arrived back at the house. Jack was separating some seeds at the table. "What's funny, Bertie?"

She told him about changing one of the Old Magger's pigs into a loaf of bread and was going to tell him about changing the farmer's pig, too. But Jack didn't

think the story about the Old Magger's pig was funny at all.

"Bertie, you shouldn't have done it."

"Aw, Jack, she's got plenty of pigs—and I was just getting back for how sister Minn's garden got rooted up."

"That's just it, Bertie. That's vengeance—getting back at someone is. Now that's a warning in the song, Bertie, and we've had enough trouble already from not being careful with the stone."

"Aw, Jack, it was only an old pig, and she deserved it."

"Bertie, even if it wasn't a warning in the song, I wouldn't mess around with the Old Magger. She's strange, Bertie. You never know what sort of bad luck she may lay on a person. Give me the stone, now, and I'll go back and change that loaf back into a pig."

"I'll *do* it, Jack, if you're going to worry and make such a fuss. But in my mind, it wouldn't hurt for somebody to change the Old Magger into a pig, if you want to know how I feel."

"Just change that loaf back, Bertie. I think it's best. It appears there's more mystery about that blue stone than we know even yet, and we ought to be real careful."

So Bertie left, and Jack set picking over the seeds and saying the song of the blue stone to himself. Presently Bertie returned.

"Did you do it, Bertie?"

"Almost, Jack. The field mice had been at the loaf, but they skitted off. Hadn't ate but just a corner off, so I said the poem and it changed into a pig all right, but he only had three legs. He got along tolerable, though, and went stumbling on back where he came from. Do you suppose that's fair enough, Jack?"

"Well, we put it right the best we could, Bertie."

Bertie started working on the seeds with Jack, and she thought about the farmer carrying his loaf of bread to the city market, and she giggled.

"What's funny, Bertie?"

"Oh, this and that, Jack." No, she wouldn't tell him about that. There was no way to correct it, and of course she had been angry when she did it, and that was warned against in the song.

Now the farmer himself hadn't noticed anything and continued on his way. He arrived in the marketplace and sold his pig at the regular place. But as he was walking away with his money, the shopkeeper uncovered the bundle and found only a loaf of bread.

"Hey! You rogue, come back here! Do you mean to sell me a loaf of bread for a pig?" He grabbed the farmer by the neck and got a stick to beat him. The man swore that it *had* been a pig, but that it had been bewitched by a woman along the King's roadway. The shopkeeper shook the money out of the farmer and beat him soundly, and gave him a little extra for telling such an outrageous story.

No one paid it much attention. It seemed that some-one was always beating someone else with a stick, and the farmer crawled into a doorway to nurse his bumps and bruises. Yet one person had noticed the whole affair. Zork, the magician to the King, had been lurking about in common clothes, eager to learn some of the subtle magic that goes on in marketplaces. This appeared to be very interesting business to him. He picked up the loaf where it had fallen aside in the scuffle and slid down next to the farmer.

"Friend," said Zork. "Is it true that a woman changed your pig into this loaf of bread?"

"True enough to get me a beating," said the man, rubbing spit onto a scraped knee.

"Could you tell me where I might find this woman?"

"I could. For the price of a pig."

"Done," said Zork and paid the man. The farmer then explained to the magician exactly where the pig had been turned into a loaf and what Bertie looked like and how they were right near the cottage path. Zork took the loaf to his quarters and called for his man.

Jack was waiting to fall asleep, hoping he might have a dream that would un-puzzle the rest of the song about the blue stone. The last lines kept running through his head:

But swallows for swallows and wings for the new,
born of the angels, the pieces are blue.

Bertie giggled, thinking of the farmer.

"What *is* funny, Bertie?"

"This and that, Jack, this and that."

But she would not have thought anything was so funny if she could have seen the man standing in a grove of trees nearby looking at the dark cottage, his eyes glinting deep in their sockets like rats in a dungeon.

Zork

Next morning, Bertie took some slops down to the pigs, and Jack was sitting around back by the garden going at his hoe with a sharpening stone. " 'Swallows for swallows,' " he muttered to himself, and kept at the hoe with smart strokes. Then to see him you might have thought he had a fit. He tossed the hoe aside and the stone up in the air and was on his feet before the stone fell and running around to the front of the cottage yelling out, "Bertie, Bertie, I got it, I got it! Bertie, Bertie, I got it!"

But Bertie was nowhere in sight. She was in a black bag on the back of a dark horse galloped by Zork's man toward the city, out of sight to Jack, over the hill, gagged and gone, no magic, but just a plain old kidnapping, or worse maybe.

Zork's man lugged the bag in the back way of the palace. He liked to keep his business secret, and had to cuff a room maid senseless to get around her and up to Zork's quarters unnoticed. He untied the bag and let it fall around Bertie. Zork made a mock bow to the lady. The man took off Bertie's gag.

"That was the most ungrateful thing that's ever happened to me!" Bertie said to Zork's man. "You come asking for directions and then stick a person in a bag when she's kind enough to help you. Don't ever ask again. I wouldn't tell you which way is up."

"Hold your tongue, woman," Zork commanded, "or I'll cut it out." He walked around Bertie, looking her over. He had a long stork-like way about him, also a sharp nose and a scraggly little head that popped up through his red cape, as if he had squeezed his head small by bearing down too hard on tiny schemes. "Bring the loaf," he ordered his man. It was set down in front of Bertie.

"Do you recognize this?" Zork asked.

"Bread is bread," Bertie said. "It all looks alike to me."

"But this loaf of bread was a pig, and it was you that changed it into this loaf. I want to know how you did that."

Bertie laughed. "A story for a nitwit," she said.

"Cut her liver out," Zork said, jerking a finger at his man.

"Oh, no!" gasped Bertie. "You wouldn't do that, would you? Oh, my, I see you would." Zork's man had his knife out and was coming up to her. "I meant no harm—it was only because I was angry at that man knocking me in the ditch. I can change the loaf back into a pig if it's so important to you. It's only a little poem what does it."

"Yes," Zork said, waving his man away. "Do that, do that." He rubbed his hands together, eager to know such powerful words. Then he would have her liver cut out.

Bertie got herself free from the bag, making some unnecessary foolery out of it so she had a chance to get the blue stone from her pocket and slip it into her mouth. Then she stood in front of the loaf and said to it:

> *The King is wise,*
> *and the Queen is pretty,*
> *and this poem might change*
> *a loaf to a piggy.*

And it did. Just like that.

"This trick I will do today before the King's eyes!" exclaimed Zork. "This is the best trick of all I've seen done! Now, woman, change it back into a loaf so I may take it to court."

Bertie thought it was unwise to do that, to give away all her magic to someone who talked so freely of cutting out her tongue and liver. So she said to him, "That is a different poem. And I won't tell you now, but I will go to court with you and stand behind a screen, and at the right time I'll tell you the poem that changes the pig back into a loaf, and then I'll leave."

Zork didn't care much for the idea. He didn't plan on letting Bertie live, but he knew he could always have her picked up afterwards, and then cut her liver out. So he agreed and most graciously sent word to the King and Queen that he would be honored to present them with a new trick that would delight and astound them.

They gathered at court, the King and Queen on their thrones and Zork before them with the pig on a small table that was dressed in a silk cloth. Behind the table was a screen, and behind the screen was Bertie. Zork's man waited outside the door with the black bag and a sharp knife. Bag, butcher, and bury Bertie was what was on his mind. Bertie peeked out through the screen. The King and Queen were dumpy and plain.

"Ahem!" said Zork. "Illustrious and magnificent sovereigns. Past many adventures, divers and strange to tell, from the mysterious East by dint of much personal sacrifice, expense, and danger, have I brought to this court—notwithstanding various and sundry entreaties from several great kings and princes elsewhere to have for their own enrichment and diversion this wondrous

and awesome show of true sorcery—have I brought before your excellent Highnesses, as I have mentioned, a
wholly extravagant, not to say incredible, and possibly
appalling . . ."

"What are you going to do with the pig?" the King
asked.

"Ahem. Well, sire, I was coming to that. I'm going
to change it into a loaf of bread."

"It better be good," said the Queen, picking her
teeth with a long fingernail.

"Yes," Zork said. "Yes, of course. A few magic words
and presto!"

"Presto," the Queen said doubtfully. "Get on with it."

Zork then made a great show of swirling his cape
around and waggling his fingers at the pig. Shielding
himself from the King and Queen behind his cape, he
stood by the screen and whispered to Bertie, "Now! Now
is the time. Tell me the words."

"Now! Now is the time. Tell me the words."

And Bertie whispered back at him:

> *The Queen is ugly,*
> *and the King is an oaf,*
> *and this poem might change,*
> *a pig to a loaf.*

Zork dropped his arm and stood looking dumbly at
the pig. "Er . . . ah. . . . erk. . . ."

"It's still a pig," said the King.

"Er . . . ahk," said Zork.

"*Those* are magic words? You sound like there's a bone stuck in your gullet," the Queen said. "And who's that behind the screen there?"

Bertie stepped out and bowed low. "Only a simple country woman, your Majesty, but one who has enough sense to know you can't change a pig into a loaf of bread. But I can take it to the kitchen and make it into a fine roast, if it please your Highnesses."

"Well said," the King declared. "And as for you, Magician, you are banished forever. Begone! And take that big rat-eyed bully with you!"

Zork rushed out, happy to get away with his head, and within the hour both he and his man were off on their separate ways out of the kingdom forever.

Bertie directed the roasting of the pig but did not stay for compliments. The workers in the kitchen wrapped her some lunch in a clean towel, and she was on the road in a short time and scampering back toward home as fast as she could go.

Jack had looked for her at all the neighbors, and had been to see sister Minn, and wandered up and down the road asking strangers if they had seen Bertie. As a last resort he went to see the Old Magger who, although she was usually reluctant to help someone in need without good payment, showed a peculiar interest in the case. One of her pigs just the day before had come back to the pen with only three legs, and she sensed something worthwhile was happening, something that might be turned to dark, secret, and perhaps profitable purposes.

The Old Magger studied the ground where Zork's man had trapped and bundled up Bertie. She prowled around, bent over at the waist, and gave her opinion.

"Rats and dungeons, Jack."

"What does that mean?"

"Nay, Jack, I can't tell you more." She had seen Bertie leading the gift pig down to sister Minn's, and now she glanced up into Jack and Bertie's slop pen and studied their new pig. "Where'd you get the new pig, Jack?"

But Jack wouldn't say. "I can't tell you that."

"Secrets, eh? Pig secrets, aye, there seems to be pig secrets about. Pig magic. Better tell, Jack, better tell the Old Magger. Three-legged pig magic, eh, Jack? Better tell the Old Magger, Jack." She crooned and took Jack by the belt. Jack broke away and ran off to the cottage.

"Snot!" said the Old Magger. She studied the new pig for a while and went back to her shack.

Jack was just leaving the cottage with a pack when Bertie came up the path. After kissing and hugging and crying a little, they sat and talked quietly about what had happened. "We was warned, Bertie," Jack said, "and maybe that's not the end of it." He had all the shutters closed, and now and then he went to the door and listened. Once he unbolted it quietly and flung it wide open.

No one was there. "The Old Magger knows something, Bertie—we've got to be careful." Then in an even quieter voice, he told Bertie that he thought he'd learned something more out of the song about the blue stone. Come morning, they would test it out.

The Swallow

Jack walked in front of Bertie down the back path to the stream and came up to the exact spot where the stone had been found.

"There, Jack," said Bertie. "There ain't no birds, let's go back."

Jack looked at a nearby group of alders. He picked up a couple of rocks and sailed them into the trees. No birds. He shrugged.

"No matter. Give us the blue stone, Bertie."

"You're a fool, Jack. Suppose a bird does fly down and eats it and flies off? Then we've lost it completely, even if we only mean to make a nice pig when we need one. I promise I'll never use it for anything else, Jack."

" 'Swallows for swallows,' " Jack said. "That means that a swallow *bird* is supposed to swallow the stone. That's what it's for, Bertie. Human beings wasn't meant to find it in the first place, nor have it and own it once they know better. It's all in the song."

"But why, Jack. What good does it do a bird?"

"That ain't up to us to know, Bertie. All we got to do is follow the song. I almost lost my head, and you almost lost your liver for trying to make something out of it we shouldn't. Give us the stone, now."

"I never want to be such a half-wit as yourself, Jack," Bertie said, but handed him the stone.

Jack took and set it down in the grass near the stream bed. He led Bertie by the arm back behind some bushes to watch. He whispered, "Remember them birds all around when we found the stone, Bertie? They was swallows. My guess is that when these blue stones fall out of heaven, all the swallows around know about it and try to get to them. But this one fell in the water and they couldn't, and had to be happy with scolding me when I found it. Now we just wait and see."

"What do you suppose will happen, Jack?"

"Can't tell, Bertie. There's still some of the song I ain't figured out yet." He said the last two lines of the song:

swallows for swallows and wings for the new,
born of the angels, the pieces are blue.

And then in a while they saw the bird. They could tell it was a swallow a good distance off, seeing its split tail and pointed wings. It came straight to the stone in a glide and landed right next to it. Then it approached, took the blue stone in its beak and tilted its head back and let the stone drop down its throat.

And there!

"Good Lord!" cried Bertie. "It changed to a *baby!*"

It had. An infant child was lying in the grass on its back, and it started to cry. Bertie snatched her shawl off as she ran to it, and had it bundled up in a minute. The baby kept crying.

"The poor thing's hungry, Jack. Go quick to sister Minn's and get some cow milk—and a bottle and a nipple."

Jack ran off, and Bertie climbed the path to the cottage. She had the baby in a blanket and was trying to hush it by rocking and singing when Jack returned with a bottle of warm milk.

"Cow was near dry," Jack said. "Tomorrow we can have all we want."

"Mercy," said Bertie, giving the baby the bottle. "The little thing's so hungry, Jack."

"I wonder should we feed it, Bertie."

"Of course we should feed it," Bertie said crossly.

"Would you let a baby cry and go hungry because it doesn't fit in with an old song? Hmmpf!"

Jack didn't have an answer to that.

"Oh, Jack, you ought to hold it. I'd never forget how it is, but every time it's just a feeling you can't remember enough about."

Jack fretted but tried not to get Bertie cross.

"Who's baby do you suppose it is, Bertie?"

Bertie looked at him sternly. "If you've got any ideas we're going to leave this baby out for the birds, Jack, you can put those ideas in that bucket and put your head in afterwards."

Those weren't Jack's ideas, and in fact he hadn't any good ideas. But he felt nervous about the baby, as if they were doing the wrong thing to keep it.

Presently the baby was finished with the milk, and Bertie laid it over her shoulder and burped it. After three hits it belched, and up came the stone and popped out of the baby's mouth onto the floor. When Bertie heard the stone hit the floor, she knew exactly what had happened, and she clutched the baby to her breast.

"It ain't changed, Jack, has it?" Bertie cried in anguish and alarm. "It ain't a pig or anything is it, Jack?"

It wasn't. It was still the same baby.

"But let up on it, Bertie. You'll squeeze the thing to death!"

"Can't, Jack—got to hold it tight so it don't have a chance to change back into a bird or something. Oh,

Jack! I can feel the dear thing trying to change back! Oh, Jack!" And she hugged the baby till it let out a grunt.

"Bertie! Bertie!" Jack cried, stepping around in front of her with his hands out wanting to do something to help. "Don't crush it so, Bertie! You'll break the little thing!"

Little by little, Bertie relaxed her hold but still clasped the baby good and firmly to her breast, and at last didn't dare let it go any farther, all the while asking Jack to watch it close if it showed any signs of wanting to change to anything else. Finally, Bertie was holding it just sort of snugged up close and could get a breath herself. She smiled and dared to pat the baby and hum to it, and it fell asleep.

"Bertie," Jack said, "now what are you going to do?"

"Look, Jack, it's sleeping. Isn't it the dearest thing you've ever seen. Oh, Jack, I won't stand for it changing back into a bird."

"You can't just hold it, Bertie."

"I've got to, Jack."

"How will you eat?"

"You can feed me, Jack."

"I can't sleep for you, Bertie. You've got to sleep."

"We'll see," said Bertie. She hummed to the baby. "All I know, Jack, is if I let it go it'll change into something else. I ain't going to let it happen, Jack."

Jack felt sure it was wrong but didn't say anything

more. He put some stew together and fed Bertie with a spoon. When the baby woke up he made some sugar water for it. Bertie held the baby all day and was holding it when Jack went to bed.

"You've got to sleep, Bertie."

"We'll see," Bertie said.

The Old Magger

Bertie was awake and cheerful in the morning.

"Go milk sister Minn's cow, Jack. The dear thing's hungry enough to eat my collar."

Jack went off to do that and returned with a bucket of milk. Bertie fed the baby.

"Ain't you tired, Bertie?"

"Never, Jack."

All day long Bertie sat in the chair with the baby, and she wouldn't let go to come to bed.

"You've got to sleep, Bertie."

"We'll see," Bertie said.

There were dark circles under Bertie's eyes the next morning. Jack watched her for hours. She wanted to talk and be talked to. She started talking about when she was just five years old and talked all day up to her tenth birthday. Jack worried for her. Now and then she started to nod, but as soon as her arms relaxed, she gripped up tight again and talked some more, sometimes droning off like she was half asleep. It came time for bed again.

"You've got to sleep, Bertie."

"We'll . . . . . . see," Bertie said.

She was awake the next morning. This would be her fourth day without sleep. She looked old and very tired. Jack decided to take the baby from her. Once, when her talking about her nineteenth year trailed off, Jack got up and put a hand on the baby.

"Don't you do it, Jack," Bertie said, without opening her eyes, and Jack sat down again and worried. If Bertie didn't sleep, she would die right there in the chair. Jack concluded that he would have to go see the Old Magger to get some magic brew that would put Bertie to sleep. He told Bertie he was going out for a while and kissed her on the forehead. He walked on down, then, and took the pig that had been made from the loaf for payment to the Old Magger.

It was smelly with pigs and worse down by the Old Magger's shack. A thin tail of smoke was coming out of the stone chimney. Jack beat his fist on the door. The

Old Magger peeked at Jack out of a side curtain, then came to the door.

"Hah!" she said, crooking a finger at Jack. "Pig magic. The pig magic man. I knew you'd come around, Jack. Heh, heh. Pig magic trouble. Them that don't know magic get in trouble with it, pig magic man. Heh, heh, heh, heh."

She was dressed in a large jacket with several pockets in it, most of them just sewed on patchwork, and all were full of little bottles and things wrapped up in paper, and scrummy little odds and ends she had gathered from the woods. A large black pot was over the fire, and in it was the three-legged pig, tied up and pouring off sweat from the heat. Jack walked round past that way and looked in on the curious affair. The pig was alive, but terribly hot and groaning, and the fumes were coming up around its head almost thick enough to choke it.

"Nevermind that," snapped the Old Magger. "That's none of your business."

Actually, she was trying to put together a brew that would make some witchery fumes to make the pig talk and tell her how it had come to lose a leg so neatly. Once, years before, she had succeeded in an experiment like this with a cat. Almost, anyway. When she had put in the last ingredient and put another stick on the fire, the cat appeared to be ready to talk. At least it looked like it wanted to say something. But then it died.

Jack preferred not to sit down. He told the Old
Magger that Bertie wouldn't go to sleep, and that what
he needed was a sleeping potion to put in her tea. The
Old Magger said that it could be done, but she wanted
to know more.

"Why won't she go to sleep, Jack? Has it to do with
pig magic?"

"I can't tell you more."

"Heh, heh, heh. People what doesn't go to sleep falls
over dead, Jack. Tell us more, Jack."

And she kept at him, so that at last Jack had to tell
her everything about the blue stone. He was too worried
about Bertie to do anything else. And the Old Magger
wanted to know everything, right from the beginning,
every single thing since they first found it, and the song
about it, and the pig poems, and everything that had
happened. Jack told her all.

"And where's the blue stone now, Jack?"

"I don't know. On the floor I suppose. Do you have
any of the sleeping potion already made up?"

"Nay, nay," said the Old Magger. "It isn't one you
make up, Jack, but one of the kind that grows in the
woods. It's a flower, a purple flower that has a closed
eye in the middle of it, and you squeeze the juice of it into
Bertie's tea and she'll sleep, Jack."

"Do you have some of these flowers?"

"Nay, but they can be got by yourself, Jack." She

walked to the window and pointed to some hills in the distance. "See, Jack, see that middle hill off there? That's the one. You go on up there and you pick those little purple flowers near the top, and then Bertie can sleep."

Jack left immediately. "Heh, heh, heh, heh," the Old Magger laughed as she watched Jack hurry off. There were no purple flowers on that hill that she knew anything about, but the journey would get Jack out of the way for a long time. When he was ten minutes gone the Old Magger went up to the cottage and looked in the open door. "Bertie?" she said. "Are you sleeping yet, Bertie?"

Bertie turned in her chair. "What do you want here? Get away from here! Scat!"

"Heh, heh. What a darling baby. Is it yours, Bertie? Heh, heh." All the time she was looking around the floor for the blue stone.

"Get out of here! Get out!"

The Old Magger spied the blue stone on the floor, and put a foot in the doorway. "Is it a sweet baby, Bertie? Does it sing like a little bird? Heh, heh, heh." Then the Old Magger made a dash and plucked the stone off the floor and was back outside the door before Bertie could move.

"Get away from here!" Bertie shouted. "Get! Get!"

"Is it soft like it's got feathers all over it, Bertie? Heh, heh, heh."

Bertie stood up and came kicking at the Old Magger, and she ran off. Bertie kicked the door shut after her. The Old Magger scatted down the hill to her shack with the blue stone wrapped inside both hands.

The Last of the Song

Jack trudged around and across the crown of the hill the Old Magger had indicated to him but found no purple flower with a closed eye in the middle of it. Weary and bush-torn he returned, opened the door and found Bertie asleep in her chair, her head lolled back, and snoring. The blanket lay half across her back and half on the floor. Her arms hung limply at her sides. The baby was gone. Jack sank to his knees in exhaustion and relief and put his head in his hands. After a couple of minutes, he got up and moved to Bertie's side and held her head up.

"Bertie, darling, you'll sleep better in bed. Come on, Bertie."

"Huh? What? Huh?" Bertie came awake slowly, but when the slightest remembrance came to her she clutched at the blanket, and then cried out for the lost baby. Dropping to the floor, she moaned as she searched through the folds of the blanket, and then she wept, and Jack sat on the floor with his arms around her.

"Oh, Jack, I let it go, I let it go! Oh, Jack, and now the dear thing's just a bird again and has flown off. Jack, I'd rather have died than to let that happen."

"I know, Bertie, I know." Jack patted her. "I know, Bertie."

There came a noise from the bedroom. It sounded like something had bumped against the window, and before Jack or Bertie could get on their feet, the baby came out of the room.

"Oh, Lord, Jack," Bertie cried. "It's got wings!"

The baby was flying up near the ceiling. It took two turns over their heads. It was smiling and holding out its arms toward them. Then it flew out the open door and up into the sky. Jack and Bertie crowded to the door and watched it fly away, higher and higher, up higher than the clouds into the blue sky, flying with the rhythm of a swallow, its pointed wings carrying it strongly, and then they could see it no more.

Jack said, " 'Swallows for swallows and wings for the newborn of the angels . . .' "

"Lord!" breathed Bertie. "A baby *angel!*"

"And that's the last of the song," Jack said.

"Thank goodness," said Bertie. "I don't think I could stand any more."

Enough

The next day Jack said, "I'd best go down to the Old Magger's and get that stone back from her before she gets in any trouble with it."

"Do what you want, Jack, but throw it back in the stream. I don't want to see it no more. The working of heaven is enough to tire a person out completely."

"Aye, it is a strange way to have babies, ain't it, Bertie?"

"Roundabout, that's the word for it, Jack."

Jack went down to the Old Magger's and was back in a few minutes. "I thought she was home," Jack said.

"Had her fire going. But when I got there I couldn't raise her. Heard some commotion inside so I looked through a window, but she wasn't there. Funny, she had some bread all set up for baking, half risen and ready to be punched down. Several loaves. But she wasn't in sight. Just some pigs in there chasing a chicken about. It flopped against the window like crazy, but I let it be. None of my business, and I wouldn't go in there without being asked." Jack mused for a bit. "Looked like them pigs was going to get that chicken, too."

"She can have the stone for all I care," Bertie said.

"Well, she knows the song about it, so I suppose anything that happens to her is her own fault."

"Aye," said Bertie. She was folding up the baby's blanket. "Jack?"

"Aye, darling?" He poured them both some tea.

"There wasn't much come of it after all, was there?"

"No gold, Bertie. No pig, either—not even a chicken or duck, finally." He set the tea out on the table for them.

"But you know, Jack, I believe it's a great blessing just to have an angel visit in your house."

"That's true, Bertie." He sipped his tea. "I suppose that's as much as there was to it."

And that's as much as there was to it.

It was enough.

It was plenty.